*For Georgie, Bethany*
*and Jemma ~ G L*

*Thanks to Mum, Dad, friends and*
*myriad family. For Brianna, Isabelle, Gabrielle,*
*Charlotte, Helena, Amy, Rachel,*
*Tim and Ange ~ L H*

LITTLE TIGER PRESS
An imprint of Magi Publications
1 The Coda Centre, 189 Munster Road, London SW6 6AW
www.littletigerpress.com

First published in Great Britain 2006
This edition published 2007

Text copyright © Gill Lewis 2006
Illustrations copyright © Louise Ho 2006

Gill Lewis and Louise Ho have asserted their rights to be identified
as the author and illustrator of this work under the Copyright, Designs
and Patents Act, 1988

Printed in Singapore by Tien Wah Press Pte.

2 4 6 8 10 9 7 5 3 1

# The
# Most Precious
# Thing

Gill Lewis

*Illustrated by* Louise Ho

LITTLE TIGER PRESS
London

Little Bear was taking Mummy Bear on a walk through the forest in the autumn sunlight. She wanted to show her the special place where the juiciest berries and the sweetest nuts could be found.

As Little Bear skipped through the rustling leaves, she suddenly spied a small blue stone glittering in the sunshine.

"Look, Mummy, look!" cried Little Bear, picking
it up. "Look at this shiny jewel I have found."
Little Bear gazed as it sparkled in her paw.
"It must be the most precious thing in the whole
wide world," she gasped.

"Oh yes, Little Bear, this is a very beautiful stone," said Mummy Bear, holding it up so that it twinkled in the light, "but the most precious thing is even prettier than this."

"Really?" said Little Bear in wonder. She
put the stone carefully in her bag. "Let's go
and look! I want to find the most precious
thing EVER!"

"Wait for me," laughed Mummy Bear, as
Little Bear scampered off through the trees.

Little Bear and Mummy Bear played games in the afternoon sun. They tried to catch the seeds that spun in the breeze. And Little Bear kept looking for something prettier than the little blue stone.

After a while they came to Little Bear's special place and they filled their tummies with juicy purple blackberries. Little Bear was reaching for a berry when she saw something pink hidden in the brambles . . .

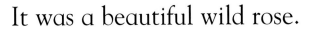

It was a beautiful wild rose.

"Mummy!" shouted Little Bear excitedly. "Come and see what I have found!"

She stroked the rose's silky petals and sniffed its sweet smell. "I've never seen such a pretty flower. Surely this must be the most precious thing?"

"This rose is very pretty, Little Bear," said Mummy Bear, "and it's soft as velvet." She tickled the rose against Little Bear's nose, making her sneeze. "But the most precious thing is even softer than this."

Little Bear wondered what on earth could be softer than her beautiful rose. She searched and searched through the dry, crunchy leaves, but she found only spiky horse chestnuts, bristly pine cones and a rather cross hedgehog!

Just then she caught sight of something fluttering high up in the trees.

"Look up there!" she shouted. "That *has* to be it!"

Mummy Bear lifted Little Bear up into the air. Caught in a spider's web was a tiny fluffy feather. Little Bear reached up high and took the feather very gently in her paw.

Little Bear touched the downy feather against her cheek.

"Oh Mummy," she whispered hopefully. "Please tell me. Is this the most precious thing?"

"It is very soft," said Mummy Bear, "but the most precious thing is even better than this – it makes me want to dance for joy."

And Mummy Bear twirled Little Bear round, making her giggle.

Little Bear was determined
to find the most precious thing.
She ran up a grassy hilltop to
look out at the woods and
fields. Hundreds of dazzling
butterflies suddenly filled the
air around her.

One of the butterflies landed
lightly on her paw. Little Bear
gazed at it in wonder.

"This is it!" she sang out
happily. "At last I have found
the most precious thing in
the whole of the big
wide world."

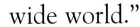

Little Bear and Mummy Bear lay in
the long grass as the butterfly fluttered
through the golden sunlight.

"Oh yes, that is very special," said
Mummy Bear softly, "but I can hold the
most precious thing safe and tight in
my arms."

"Oh, please tell me what it is!"
said Little Bear crossly. "I have looked
absolutely everywhere and I still
haven't found it."

Mummy Bear smiled. "The most precious thing is prettier than any jewel, is softer than a rose or the fluffiest feather, and fills me with more joy than a dancing butterfly. The most precious thing . . ." she said, hugging Little Bear tightly, ". . . is you!"

# Precious books for every day from Little Tiger Press

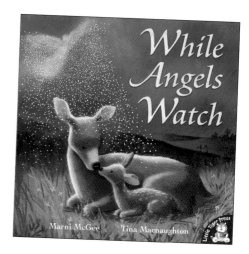

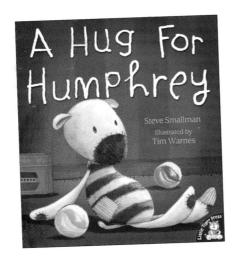

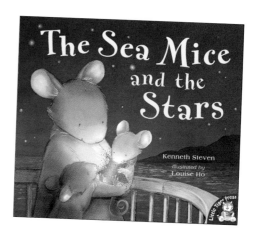

For information regarding any of the above titles
or for our catalogue, please contact us:
Little Tiger Press, 1 The Coda Centre,
189 Munster Road, London SW6 6AW, UK
Tel: 020 7385 6333
Fax: 020 7385 7333
E-mail: info@littletiger.co.uk
www.littletigerpress.com